The adventures of Feefeen and Friends

Feefeen MacRageen is a real furry teddy bear. He lives with his owner Barbara in Dublin. When nobody is looking, he gets up to some pretty exciting adventures. In this book, Barbara tells six of his stories. If you have a teddy bear, do you know what he gets up to when you are not looking?

The adventures of Feefeen and Friends

Barbara Naughton
Illustrated by Declan Considine

First published in Ireland in 2012
by Furry Books
an imprint of Universal Humourous Publishing.
Dublin, Ireland.

Text © Barbara Naughton 2012
Illustrations © Declan Considine 2012. www.con.ie

All rights reserved. No part of this book may be reproduced, stored in a retrieval system, or transmitted, in any form or by any means, electronic, mechanical, photocopying, recording or otherwise, without the prior permission of Universal Humourous Publishing.

Printed in Ireland by Gemini International Ltd.

Universal Humourous Publishing
Registered in Ireland No. 460909B

ISBN 978-0-9575814-1-8

I would like to thank
Aoife Barrett for her editorial work
on Feefeen's stories.
I would also like to thank Alison O'Reilly,
Patrice Harrington and Niamh O'Connor
for their helpful comments and feedback.
Finally, I would like to thank Declan Considine
for his wonderful artwork.

Barbara Naughton

Contents

Feefeen and the Twins	9
Feefeen and the Circus	25
Feefeen and the New Teacher	41
Feefeen and the Haunted House	59
Feefeen and the Hot Air Balloon	77
Feefeen and the Dolphins	93

Feefeen
and the Twins

It was summertime and the birds had returned to the village of Salmonswood, where the MacRageen family lived.

One morning, Feefeen MacRageen was playing on the old rope swing in their front garden. He was a five-year-old bear cub, with brown eyes and brown fur.

Feefeen and his sister, Dolleen, were pushing each other on the swing.

"Look Dolleen! It's Aunt Cipeen," Feefeen grinned.

"She still has her old, green car," Dolleen smiled.

"And look our cousins, Tribbin and Cribbin, are in the back seat," Feefeen shouted, waving at them.

"Feefeen you run in and tell Mameen that they're here!" Dolleen said. "I'll help them with their cases."

"Okay," Feefeen said.

He ran back inside.

"Mameen, Mameen!" he shouted.

"Sshh Feefeen! Don't shout," Mameen said.

"Aunt Cipeen and the twins are here," Feefeen whispered, laughing.

Mameen started laughing too.

"Come on, we'll go and meet them. Feefeen watch where you are going. I don't want you to fall and hurt yourself," Mameen said.

"I will walk on my tippy-toes Mameen," he grinned.

"Hello Lavender," Mameen's sister, Cipeen, shouted. She waved at them from the front gate.

"Hello Cipeen and children," Mameen smiled and hugged them.

"Hello Aunt Lavender," the twins whispered.

"The twins are very quiet today. Usually they never stop yapping," Aunt Cipeen smiled.

"If they are anything like their father I'm surprised they ever stay quiet," Mameen said.

They all burst out laughing.

I will be back to collect you two tomorrow," Cipeen said to the twins. "Now behave yourselves and no mischief."

"I'm sure Feefeen and Dolleen can keep them busy. Have fun at the wedding. Say hello to everybody for me," Mameen said.

"I will of course. See you in the morning," Aunt Cipeen said.

She jumped back into her old, green car.

Everybody waved as she drove off.

"Well children would you like some lunch?" Mameen asked the twins.

"Yes please Aunt Lavender," Tribbin and Cribbin smiled.

The five bears walked into the kitchen. Dolleen showed the twins their beds while Feefeen helped Mameen set the table.

Then Mameen started to make lunch. They had loads of gorgeous food. They all loved blackberries and salmon.

"Aunt Lavender can we go out and play on the swing?" Cribbin asked after lunch.

"Of course you can. Feefeen, bring your cousins

outside. Make sure to give them a good big push," Mameen said.

"Come on Cribbin and Tribbin. Follow me," Feefeen said, running out the door.

The twins rushed after him. Tribbin jumped on the swing.

"Feefeen, push me, push me," he said.

Then Tribbin jumped off and Cribbin got on.

"Feefeen, will you give me a really good push?" Cribbin asked.

"Of course," Feefeen said.

He pushed the swing really hard.

"Weeee; Weeee; Weeee. This is great. It's like flying in the sky," Cribbin screamed. "Come on Feefeen, you have a go now."

Feefeen jumped on the swing.

Tribbin and Cribbin looked at each other and grinned. They were going to play a joke on Feefeen. The two of them gave the swing a huge push.

"Ahhhhh!" Feefeen shouted.

"Would you like to go even higher, Feefeen?" Cribbin asked.

"No Cribbin, I feel sick," Feefeen said. "Stop pushing the swing."

"You want to go even higher?" Cribbin asked. He was pretending he couldn't hear Feefeen.

"Nooooooo!" Feefeen yelled, as he flew higher into the air. "Stoooopppp!"

The twins giggled. They thought Feefeen sounded really funny. Tribbin was in fits of laughter.

"Let me down! Dolleen! Dolleen! Help," Feefeen

screamed. He was scared.

The twins heard Dolleen coming. They grabbed the swing and helped Feefeen to get off.

"Feefeen, I am very sorry. I had no idea you really wanted me to stop the swing," Cribbin said. "It was only a joke."

"It didn't feel like a joke to me!" Feefeen groaned.

Dolleen ran over.

"Feefeen, I thought I heard you screaming. You were going very high on the swing. Are you okay?" she asked.

Feefeen didn't want to get his cousins in trouble.

"I just got a bit of a fright," he said. "I feel dizzy."

"Wasn't it exciting?" Tribbin asked.

"No, it was scary. I thought I was going to fall," Feefeen groaned again.

"If I catch anyone pushing the swing that high again I will tell Mameen," Dolleen said. "You need to be more careful."

"We promise we will be careful," Cribbin and Tribbin said.

They all walked back into the kitchen. Mameen was making cakes.

"Did Feefeen show you the swing?" she asked.

"Yes Aunt Lavender," Cribbin laughed.

"It was wonderful," Tribbin grinned.

Feefeen and Dolleen did not say anything.

"Your mother told me that you go hiking and climbing every week," Mameen said.

"Yes that's true Aunt Lavender. We love walking in the woods and going fishing," Tribbin said.

"Well Salmonswood Forest is near here. It is a very big forest with many streams. I'm sure if you use your noses you might come across a salmon. Feefeen, will you give your cousins a tour of the forest?" Mameen asked.

"Yes, Mameen," Feefeen mumbled.

He wasn't happy. The twins made him nervous.

"Mameen can Dolleen come with us?" he asked.

"Dolleen is helping me at home today," Mameen said.

"Why can't she come with us?"

Feefeen was cross. He didn't want to be left on his own with his cousins.

"Go on Feefeen, take your cousins to the forest," Mameen ordered.

After a short walk in the summer sunshine they arrived at the wooden gates of Salmonswood Forest.

"It is huge, Feefeen. Your mother wasn't joking when she said it was the biggest forest in Salmonswood. It is probably the biggest forest in the world," Tribbin shouted.

"It must be full of salmon," Cribbin grinned. He loved eating salmon. It was his favourite fish.

They went into the forest. Feefeen began to run around the trees, playing hide and seek.

"Where are you Feefeen?" Tribbin shouted.

"You have to find me," Feefeen laughed.

The twins found him and they chased each other around the trees.

"I love jumping in the streams and sometimes I go

swimming," Feefeen said.

The sunlight began to fade and the bear cubs could hear strange noises in the woods. They could hear the owls and other birds calling: "Whoooooo, whoooo, whoooo,, tweet, tweet, quack, quack."

"I am going to have a rest," Feefeen said, panting. The twins sat beside him.

"I'm very thirsty after all that playing. I need a drink of water. Feefeen where is the nearest stream?" Cribbin asked.

"It's just behind those trees."

They walked to the stream and got a big drink.

"We'll have to be careful. Farmer Crank has salmon nets on this stream and he doesn't like strangers," Feefeen said.

"Where are the nets?" Cribbin asked.

"At the top of the stream – where the salmon jump," Feefeen said. "The salmon jump into the nets and then they are caught!"

"Can you show us?" Tribbin asked.

They walked to a small waterfall.

"See, that is where the salmon jump. Farmer Crank's nets are there," Feefeen explained.

Tribbin walked into the middle of the waterfall. He lifted up a net full of salmon.

"Dinner is served," he laughed.

"They're Farmer Crank's salmon Tribbin. He'll be very cross if he sees us eating his fish," Feefeen said.

Cribbin walked into the water and lifted up another net.

"He has loads of salmon Feefeen. He won't miss

a few!"

Feefeen didn't want to fight with his cousins. They were bigger than him.

The twins walked out of the water and dropped the two nets full of salmon on the ground.

Feefeen didn't want any salmon. He put the nets back after the twins had eaten three salmons each. Cribbin and Tribbin were very noisy eaters.

"That was fun. All we need now is some honey. I love honey," Tribbin said.

"I love honey too. I know where we could find three, big jars of honey," Feefeen said. He really wanted some honey.

"Wonderful! Where?" Tribbin asked.

"Farmer Crank has the sweetest jars of honey in Salmonswood. Some bears say he talks to the bees. He keeps the jars outside his house. Taking them will not be easy. He might catch us and we'll get into big trouble," Feefeen warned. "He lives over that hill."

"Feefeen, he won't catch us," Cribbin laughed.

"We'll run away if he sees us," Tribbin grinned.

Feefeen knew it was a bad thing to do but he LOVED honey.

The three young bears crawled to the top of the hill. On the other side they could see Farmer Crank's wooden cabin.

"Oh no!" Feefeen gasped. "Farmer Crank is outside. He's chopping wood."

"He looks angry," Tribbin said.

"Where are his honey pots?" Cribbin asked.

"At the back of the house," Feefeen whispered.

Feefeen felt bad. He wanted to run away but he also wanted some honey. He wished the twins hadn't come to stay.

"If we creep around the back of his house he won't see us. We can stuff our bellies and Farmer Crank won't know," Tribbin said.

They crawled around the house. Feefeen saw Farmer Crank stop and sniff the air.

"Stop! I saw his nose twitching. I think he can smell us," Feefeen whispered.

They waited and Farmer Crank went into the cabin.

"Ok Feefeen you are the lookout. Cribbin and I will sneak down and grab the honey. If Farmer Crank moves, you have to whistle," Tribbin said.

"Ok," Feefeen whispered.

Tribbin and Cribbin slowly crawled towards the honey pots. They were nearly there when they heard a whistle. Farmer Crank was running towards them.

"Ahhhh!" they shouted.

Feefeen was already running away. Cribbin and Tribbin rushed after him.

Farmer Crank chased them but they were faster. He gave up and went back to his cabin.

"What a wonderful adventure," Cribbin grinned.

"I thought he was going to catch us," Tribbin smiled.

Feefeen was worried. Farmer Crank had seen him.

"We better go home. It'll be dark soon," he said.

They ran home and went into the kitchen.

"Hi, Aunt Lavender," Tribbin grinned.

"We had a wonderful afternoon – all thanks to Feefeen," Cribbin laughed.

But Mameen didn't smile. She looked upset.

"Sorry we are late home, Mameen," Feefeen said.

"Feefeen we have a visitor. He is in the sitting-room and he wants to speak to you and Cribbin and Tribbin," Mameen said.

The three cubs looked at each other. They slowly followed Mameen into the sitting-room.

Farmer Crank was the visitor.

"Hello cubs," Farmer Crank said.

They tried to hide behind Mameen.

"Stealing salmon, breaking Farmer Crank's nets and then trying to steal his honey pots. I'm shocked. Would somebody like to explain?" Mameen asked. "Have you anything to say to Farmer Crank?"

The cubs looked down at the ground.

"I'm very sorry Farmer Crank," Feefeen said.

"We're sorry Farmer Crank," Cribbin and Tribbin said.

"It is very bad to steal. You should never take anything that doesn't belong to you," Farmer Crank said.

"We're sorry," the cubs said.

"Well Feefeen, you will get no pocket-money for the next three months. I have given it to Farmer Crank to pay for the salmon. And Tribbin and Cribbin I will tell your mother about this when I see her tomorrow morning. Now go to bed and there's no supper for any of you," Mameen said.

She was very cross.

Feefeen undressed and jumped into bed. He felt very sad. He wished he hadn't told his cousins about the salmon and the honey. He was so tired he quickly fell asleep.

He dreamt that Farmer Crank was chasing him. Then a noise woke him up. Feefeen started shaking. There were two ghosts at the end of his bed.

"We have come to take you away Feefeen Macrageen," the first ghost said.

"There is Nooooooo escape," the second ghost wailed.

Feefeen pulled the bedclothes over his head.

"What have I done?" Feefeen cried.

"You have been a wicked bear. You helped steal Farmer Crank's salmon," the first ghost said.

"I didn't eat any," Feefeen whispered.

"You are a thief Feefeen MacRageen. We have to take you awaaayyyyy!" the second ghost howled.

Feefeen was very scared.

Suddenly the bedroom door opened and Dolleen switched on the light. She grabbed the two ghosts and pulled off their sheets.

Tribbin and Cribbin were the ghosts!

Feefeen's head popped out from under the bedclothes.

Dolleen grabbed the twins by the ears. "You're very bad bears!" she said.

"We are sorry. We were only playing a game,"

Tribbin said.

"Scaring Feefeen is not a game. You have caused enough trouble. Now go back to bed before I call Mameen," Dolleen said.

"Sorry Feefeen," the twins grinned and left.

"Dolleen, you are the best sister in the world," Feefeen smiled.

"Feefeen you have never stolen anything in your life before. The sooner our cousins are gone, the better," Dolleen said. "Would you like me to leave the light on?"

"No, I'm okay now Dolleen. I know there won't be any more ghosts!"

The next day, Aunt Cipeen parked outside the picket fence. Mameen and the twins were waiting for her.

"Hi Cipeen, you're up bright and early. Did you enjoy the wedding?" Mameen asked.

"Oh Lavendar it was a lovely day. I'm glad I didn't miss it. Thank you for minding the twins for me. Did they get up to any mischief?"

"They got into trouble stealing fish from Farmer Crank. Hopefully this is the last time they'll ever do it. I am not giving Feefeen any pocket money for three months because I paid Farmer Crank for the fish."

"I'm so sorry Lavendar. I will make sure they do not get a penny from me for three months either," Cipeen said. "Get into the car you two trouble-makers!"

"Mammy we are very sorry," Cribbin and Tribbin said. They wished they hadn't eaten the salmon.

"We'll talk about it later. We'd better go now. We have a long drive back to Grizzly Peaks," Cipeen said. "Bye Lavender!"

Mameen waved goodbye.

In the sitting-room Feefeen and Dolleen watched as Aunt Cipeen and the twins drove off.

"Yippee! No more Cribbin and Tribbin playing jokes on me and getting me into trouble," Feefeen said. "Yippee!"

Feefeen and Dolleen danced around the room they were so happy.

Feefeen
and the Circus

One Sunday morning, Feefeen MacRageen lay fast asleep in his bed.

He was a small, brown bear and he was hidden under the three duvets covering his bed.

Feefeen loved sleeping. Sunday was his favourite day of the week because his Mameen let him have a long sleep.

It was nearly 11 o'clock when Mameen woke him: "Come on Feefeen, it's time to get up!"

Feefeen slowly woke up. He opened his big, brown eyes. He was very hungry. "Mameen, what's for breakfast?" he asked.

"I am making your favourite – pancakes. They'll be ready in five minutes. Hurry up now!" Mameen said.

She went back downstairs.

Feefeen jumped out of bed. He put on his favourite blue dungarees and ran down to the kitchen.

He sat at the table beside his sister Dolleen. She had a pink bow in her hair. He pulled it and laughed.

"Feefeen, stoooopp! Mameen, I love your pancakes," Dolleen grinned, looking at Feefeen.

She was spreading loads of lovely, golden honey on her pancake.

Feefeen's tummy rumbled.

"Give me a bite Dolleen. Pleeeeessee!" he said.

"No, Feefeen you will have to wait," Dolleen said.

"Dolleen, you are so mean. I'm hungry," Feefeen groaned.

Luckily, Mameen put a pancake on his plate before there was a fight.

"Dolleen, please pass the honey," Feefeen said

She passed it to him and grinned. When he put his knife into the honey pot, it was all gone.

"Mameen, Dolleen has eaten all the honey. Do we have another pot?" Feefeen asked.

"Mameen I have not eaten all the honey. If Feefeen got out of bed earlier there would have been honey for him. It's not my fault he is a lazy bear," Dolleen said.

"I am not lazy Dolleen. Sundays are for sleeping," Feefeen growled. He was cross. He had to eat his pancake without any honey. "Where's Dad?"

"He is in the sitting-room," Mameen answered.

Feefeen made a face at Dolleen and left the kitchen.

He found his Dad, Bumble, reading a book.

"Hi, Dad, what is the book about?" Feefeen asked.

"Morning, Feefeen! I am reading a family book about Angus MacRageen," Bumble smiled.

"Who was Angus MacRageen?"

"Angus was your great-great-Grandfather. He was the most fearsome bear that ever lived in Salmonswood!"

"Did you ever meet Angus?"

"Sadly no, but your grandfather did. I'm sure he will tell you many stories about Angus if you ask him."

"I would love to hear those stories. I'll ask him at Christmas," Feefeen grinned.

They both looked up as Mameen came in.

"Feefeen, Dolleen and I are going to McGoogle's store. Would you like to come?" she asked.

"Yes please Mameen!" Feefeen said. "Bye Dad, I hope you have some good stories to tell me when you finish the book!"

Mameen drove to McGoogle's shop.

"Good morning, Lavender. Hello Dolleen, Feefeen," Peeble McGoogle smiled, as they walked in.

"Good morning Peeeble," Mameen replied.

Mameen, Dolleen and Feefeen were busy shopping when they heard a voice outside.

"Roll up, roll up! The circus has arrived in town, for one performance only, this afternoon at 3 o'clock. Roll up, roll up! Come and see Keebie Monstrous and his crazy clowns."

Feefeen and Dolleen ran to the door. Two clowns were sitting in an aeroplane-shaped car outside the shop. They rushed over to it.

"Hello, little bears," the clown said. Her name was Polly. She gave Dolleen a bunch of flowers. Dolleen bent down to smell them and they exploded in a puff of powder.

Feefeen burst out laughing.

"Ha, ha Dolleen your face is all white."

Dolleen started laughing too

"Would you like to come to the circus this afternoon?" Polly asked.

"Ooooh yes," Dolleen nodded.

Mameen came out of the shop.

"Mameen, Mameen can we go to the circus?" Dolleen asked.

"Mameen, Mameen, can we pleassseeee go to the

circus?" Feefeen shouted.

The other clown handed Mameen a bunch of flowers but they didn't explode

"I really hope that you will be able to attend our performance this afternoon," he said.

Then he jumped into the car and the clowns drove away, honking the horn.

"What lovely flowers!" Mameen said.

"May we go Mameeneen?" Dolleen and Feefeen pleaded.

"Of course we can," Mameen answered. "Let's go home and tell your Dad."

When they got home, Dolleen and Feefeen jumped out of the car. They ran into the house.

"Dad the circus has arrived in town," Dolleen shouted.

"Mameen said we could go!" Feefeen yelled. "Will you bring us?"

"Of course I will bring you. Let me see if there is anything in Angus's book about circuses," Bumble said.

Feefeen was too excited to wait. He ran over to his friends' house and told Toonie and Tawney all about the circus.

Toonie and Tawney ran inside and asked their Dad if they could go too.

"Dolleen and Feefeen are going. We will be the only bears in Salmonswood not there," Toonie pleaded.

"I am working this afternoon," Tiberius MacGrew,

their Dad answered. "If Bumble will bring you, I will pay for the tickets."

Within seconds, they had raced over to ask Bumble.

"Oh Mr MacRageen, our father is working this afternoon so he can't bring us to the circus. But he said we can go if you will take us. Can we please go with you?" Toonie asked.

"Say yes Dad!" Feefeen pleaded.

"We would be no trouble, Mr MacRageen," Tawney smiled.

"Of course I will take you. We will collect you on the way," Bumble answered.

"Thank you so much!" Toonie and Tawney grinned.

"Hurray!" Feefeen yelled.

In a field in the middle of Salmonswood, the circus animals were busy putting up the Big Top. Their boss, Keebie Monstrous, was an angry Tasmanian Dust Devil.

"Lift those tents. Hurry, hurry – the show has to be ready to start at 3 o'clock. Lift those poles you two or there will be no supper tonight," he roared at the two elephants.

Keebie walked to his caravan. A black rat, named Ratty, met him there.

"Boss we have sold 120 tickets already and we hope to sell another 200," Ratty said.

"Excellent Ratty. Wake me when the Big Top is ready. And make sure there is no slacking or there will be no food for any of you," Keebie said, with a mean laugh.

Just before 3 o'clock, all the bears got into Bumble's car and drove to MacPlooden's field.

When they got there, Feefeen put down the window and pointed at everything. They were all very excited.

Look there is an ice-cream van," he said, "and two elephants!"

"Feefeen be careful you don't fall out!" Dad laughed as he parked the car.

They all ran up to the ice-cream van.

"Good afternoon folks. What flavour would you like?" the owl behind the counter asked.

"Do you have anything with Honey in it?" Dolleen asked.

"I have munchin honey and banana boat vanilla," Mr Owl replied.

I'd love to have one," Dolleen smiled.

"I would like the pumkalink strawberry flick Mr Owl,' Bumble said.

"I would love to try the tackelberry chuckaloo," Feefeen said.

"We'll have that too!" Tawney and Toonie laughed.

"I will try the green grass pipers with vanilla," Mameen said.

The Owl handed everyone their ice-creams. They were all very odd shapes.

"Thank you Mr Owl," they all said.

"I hope you enjoy our show," Mr Owl smiled.

The circus was about to start.

Keebie, the Ringmaster, came out.

"Welcome to the show and thank you all for coming!"

Two clowns ran out. Everyone cheered when they jumped on a one-wheeled bike. The two clowns, Pippy and Polly, cycled around the ring until they fell off. Then Polly stood on Pippy's shoulders.

"He must be very strong," Feefeen said.

A third clown came in. He was driving a car covered with balloons. There was a parrot in a cage on top of the car. The driver beeped the horn and Pippy and Polly fell down.

All the bear cubs giggled.

Then Pippy the clown ran behind the car. He pushed a potato into the exhaust pipe. The car spluttered and stopped.

The driver lifted up the bonnet. He looked at the engine and scratched his head.

"I don't know what's wrong with my car. Why won't it go?" he shouted.

Everybody in the audience pointed to the back of the car. "There's a potato in the back of the car," they shouted.

The clown walked to the back of the car to look for the potato and Polly hit him over the head with a joke hammer. The driver fell down and everybody burst out laughing.

Two more clowns ran in with a stretcher. They put him on it and carried him out.

Feefeen was still laughing when a pink elephant

suddenly came in. The two clowns ran off

"It's Bekki, our special pink elephant," Keebie announced.

"Oh look at the pink elephant," Feefeen grinned.

The elephant walked around the ring. She was sniffing the audience with her long nose. She came to Feefeen and gave him a kiss.

Feefeen beamed with joy. "I love the circus," he laughed.

Everybody cheered and the elephant left.

Three giant mice rushed in.

Everybody gasped. They were huge.

"Mameen, I have to go to the toilet," Feefeen said.

"Ok Feefeen, off you go but come straight back," she said.

Feefeen quickly walked towards the woods. He didn't want to miss any of the show. He passed a caravan and saw Bekki, the pink elephant. Keebie, the Ringmaster, was giving out to her. He was holding a stick.

"I want you to stay in the ring for 10 minutes," Keebie yelled. "If you don't I will hit you with this stick."

"I am tired and hungry," Bekki replied.

"I am the boss. And you will do as I tell you.... or else," he glared.

Keebie left and went back into the Big Top.

Feefeen walked over to Bekki and sat beside her.

"Why do you let him treat you so badly?" Feefeen asked.

Bekki was trembling.

"I'm afraid," she said.

"But you are so big and strong. I don't understand"

"Although I am much bigger than Keebie, I am a gentle creature. I don't like fighting with anyone."

"Even if they are going to hurt you?"

Suddenly they heard Keebie's voice: "Bekki, come here at once."

"Don't listen to him and please don't go. He is only trying to bully you," Feefeen pleaded.

Bekki turned and walked away.

Feefeen headed towards the bushes. Then he rushed back inside. He felt very sorry for Bekki.

As Feefeen sat back down Keebie Monstrous came into the ring.

"And now for your entertainment – The World's Strongest Bear, the Great Maximus, all the way from the North Pole," Keebie yelled.

A huge, white bear walked into the middle of the ring.

"Rooooaaaarrrr!" he shouted.

Some of the cubs hid behind their parents.

Keebie left the ring as Maximus began his display of strength.

"Dolleen that Keebie is a bully. I saw him saying he would hit Bekki with a stick," Feefeen said.

"Are you sure Feefeen?" Dolleen asked.

"Come and ask Bekki yourself if you don't believe me."

They checked Mameen was busy watching the

show.

"Come on," Feefeen whispered.

The two bears silently crept out of the tent. Toonie and Tawney saw them leaving and followed them.

Feefeen led Dolleen to the caravan. Keebie was shouting at Bekki again.

"Bekki you are going back out on that stage whether you like it or not. If you don't, I will not feed you for a week," Keebie shouted.

"Why are you such a cruel creature?" Bekki asked.

"Yes, why are you so cruel?" Feefeen asked. He made his voice sound big and strong.

For a second Keebie was frightened. Then he saw Feefeen was only a five-year-old bear cub.

"This is none of your business little bear," Keebie said.

Dolleen came and stood beside Feefeen.

"You are nothing but a small, nasty bully who is cruel to poor Bekki," Dolleen said.

Keebie was a bit afraid of the two bears. He saw Ratty and Batty nearby.

"Ratty, come here," Keebie shouted.

They rushed over.

"Ratty, please escort our two young circus-goers back to the Big Top," Keebie said.

Ratty immediately grabbed Dolleen and Feefeen by the shoulders.

Dolleen was very cross.

"Our father is the police sergeant in Salmonswood. When we tell him about you and Bekki you will be in big trouble. He will soon close your circus," she said.

"Ratty, Batty, grab those two and put them in the cage behind my caravan," Keebie said.

Bekki was too afraid to help the cubs.

Toonie and Tawney were hiding behind a fence. They watched Batty and Ratty taking their friends to the cage.

"Let us go you bully. Help! You won't get away with it Help!" Feefeen and Dolleen shouted.

Batty and Ratty threw a cloth over the cage and went to find Keebie.

As soon as they were out of sight, Toonie and Tawney ran over. They lifted the cloth and whispered: "Can we get you out?"

"No, run and tell our Dad what's happened," Dolleen said. "Oh no! Watch out!"

Toonie and Tawney turned around. Ratty and Batty were standing behind them.

"Ahhhh," Toonie gasped.

"Run!" Tawney shouted.

"Quick grab them," Ratty said.

Ratty and Batty chased after them.

Toonie and Tawney ran faster.

"Got you!" Ratty said. "Owwww!"

As Ratty grabbed the two cubs, Bekki knocked him over.

"Thanks Bekki," Toonie and Tawney said and ran into the Big Top. There was a break in the show and the ring was empty. Mr and Mrs MacRageen were buying popcorn and sweets. Toonie and Tawney

rushed over.

"Mr MacRageen! Feefeen and Dolleen have been taken prisoner by the evil Keebie Monstrous. Quick, come and help them," Tawney panted.

"Slow down. You are not making sense," Bumble said.

Toonie took a deep breath.

"We followed Dolleen and Feefeen outside. They went to the caravans and we saw Keebie taking Dolleen and Feefeen prisoner," Toonie said.

"Well, you better take us to them and we'll find out what's going on," he said.

They followed Toonie and Tawney out of the Big Top.

"It's just here Mr MacRageen," Toonie said.

They walked around the corner. Keebie, Maximus, Ratty and Batty blocked their way.

"Good afternoon. The caravan compound is off limits to all circus-goers," Keebie said.

"I am the Police Sergeant in Salmonswood. Nowhere is off-limits to me. Now let me pass," Bumble answered.

"Get him Maximus," Keebie shouted.

Bumble grabbed Maximus's arm and turned him upside down. The big, white bear hit the ground. Ratty and Batty ran away.

"You can't go in there," Keebie said. He was scared. He saw Bekki the elephant coming over. "Bekki, these bears are causing a nuisance. Throw them out!"

"No, I won't help you. You're a bully. These bears are trying to help me," Bekki replied. "Your cubs are over here. They are very brave. You must be very proud of them."

Bekki led them to Feefeen and Dolleen. Bumble opened up the lock.

Feefeen ran over to Bekki and gave her a big hug.

"Thank you so much. You are the best elephant in this circus. You stood up to that horrible bully Keebie," Feefeen said.

"He won't ever be able to hurt you again," Dolleen smiled.

"I couldn't have done it without your help!" Bekki said. "I have allowed Keebie to bully all of us for too long. I will be our leader now and I will make sure everybody is treated well."

She wrapped her trunk around Feefeen and Dolleen. Then she lifted them up onto her back.

"Yippee!" they shouted.

"Well, the show must go on. Would you like to see the last act?" Bekki asked.

"Of course we would," Mameen smiled.

Bekki lifted Dolleen and Feefeen off her back. Then she led all the bears back into the Big Top.

"Dad, I think I want to be a clown when I grow up," Feefeen shouted.

Everybody burst out laughing.

Feefeen
and the New Teacher

Feefeen was dreaming about honey when the cold woke him up. Dolleen had dragged all the bedclothes off his bed.

"Feefeen, we have a new teacher today. You have to get up," Dolleen said.

Feefeen curled up in a ball.

"Mean sister," he mumbled.

"Get up!" Dolleen said, as she went downstairs.

"Learn this.... learn that. I bet he will give us homework on the first night," Feefeen grumbled, getting dressed.

Two minutes later, Feefeen ran into the kitchen.

"Now Feefeen, you be a good bear today. And no playing tricks on the new teacher," Mameen said.

"Would I do that?" he grinned.

"Yes you would Feefeen. Now hurry up. I don't want to be late," Dolleen said.

She walked over and kissed Mameen goodbye.

Feefeen grabbed his toast and his schoolbag and followed her out the door.

They soon arrived outside the school gates, where they met Feefeen's best friends, Toonie and Tawney.

"Hi Feefeen! Did you hear our new teacher was once a famous magician?" Toonie grinned.

"A famous magician? Who told you that Toonie?" Feefeen asked.

"Cedric Longsnout."

"Cedric Longsnout is the biggest storyteller that has ever lived in Salmonswood. He is always making up stories. Teachers are not magicians," Dolleen said.

"I bet you're wrong!" Toonie grinned.

As they walked into their classroom a paper aeroplane hit Feefeen on the nose. All the bears were running around and the blackboard was covered in scribbles.

A few seconds later, the door opened and the new teacher walked in.

"Good morning cubs my name is Mr Biggles. Please be seated," he said, putting on his glasses.

All the young bears flew into their seats.

"I will be your teacher for one week and then Mrs Crabpaw will be back. I hope to teach you many interesting lessons," he said.

He placed a book on each desk.

"Cubs, please open on page 14, 'The Magician and the Princess'," Mr Biggles said.

He glanced around the classroom and looked at a cub with a long nose. "And who might you be?" he asked.

"Cedric Longsnout, sir."

"The right name for you I think," Mr Biggles smiled.

Cedric grinned and the other cubs burst out laughing. Cedric was very proud of his long nose.

"Start reading please," Mr Biggles said.

The story was very good and the time flew by.

At 12 pm the lunch bell rang. All the bears ran out into the schoolyard. Feefeen, Dolleen, Toonie and Tawney began playing chasing.

"What do you think of our new teacher?" Feefeen asked.

"He seems very nice," Dolleen said.

"He's not bossy like Mrs Crabpaw," Tawney added.

"I wonder if he will do some magic," Toonie said.

"Toonie, Mr Biggles is a teacher, not a magician," Dolleen said.

"I'll be back in a minute," Feefeen said. He walked to the classroom window and peeped inside.

"Wow!" Feefeen whispered. Four books were floating in the air. Mr Biggles was at his desk holding a weird necklace. It was flashing brightly. Feefeen ducked down. He didn't want Mr Biggles to see him.

"I'll tell the others on the way home," Feefeen muttered, as the lunch break ended.

Feefeen was bursting with excitement when the bell rang that afternoon. They started walking home and he told Toonie and Tawney what he'd seen.

"Stop telling tales," Dolleen said.

"Dolleen I saw the books flying in the air!" Feefeen shouted.

"Stop it Feefeen. You are always making up stories. I suppose Mr Biggles has a broom and flies on it as well," she said.

"He probably does," Feefeen said. "I don't think he's a magician. I think he's a witch."

"We'll see you later," Tawney and Toonie said.

Feefeen and Dolleen were still arguing when they walked into their kitchen.

"Hi cubs, did you enjoy your first day with your new teacher?" Mameen asked.

"Mameen, Mr Biggles is a great teacher," Dolleen smiled.

"Mr Biggles is a witch," Feefeen shouted.

"Witches are normally girls Feefeen," Mameen smiled.

"Well, he is a boy-witch then!"

"Do you mean a wizard Feefeen? But there are no such things as wizards or witches," Mameen said.

"There are. I saw Mr Biggles make some books float across the room. He has a magic necklace thing. It was shining really brightly."

"I thought wizards had magic wands not magic necklace things or do you mean an amulet?" Dolleen laughed.

"Dolleen, don't be teasing your little brother. Feefeen, your new teacher is not a wizard. Now, would you like jam or honey sandwiches?" Mameen asked.

"Why does nobody ever believe me?" Feefeen asked.

"It might have something to do with the time you told us pirates had stolen your boat from the pond or the time you told us the school was on fire," Dolleen chuckled.

Mameen started laughing too.

"I will show you Dolleen. Mr Biggles is a wizard and I will prove it," Feefeen said.

After dinner, Feefeen walked over to talk to Toonie and Tawney. He told them that he had a plan and he needed their help.

"Of course we'll help you," Toonie said.

"I want to see him do some magic too," Tawney grinned.

"We'll make Dolleen say she's sorry," Feefeen said. "I'll go and find my Dad's binoculars. See you later."

It took Feefeen a while to find the binoculars. It was dark when he sneaked down the stairs. He opened the front door and whistled quietly. Toonie and Tawney were waiting for him. They were both dressed in dark clothes and were wearing eye masks.

"Did you bring the torch Tawney?" Feefeen asked.

"Yes and some rope in case we need it."

As they tip-toed away, they didn't know Dolleen was watching them.

"Feefeen can look after himself this time," she muttered and went back to bed.

When the three cubs arrived at the school, there was a light shining inside. They crept to their classroom window and slowly pushed it open. Then they climbed inside.

"Now remember, we need to be very careful," Feefeen hissed.

The bears slowly walked across their classroom. They kept bumping into things. Just before they moved into the corridor, they stopped and listened.

"We are looking for the magic necklace thing – the amulet that was around Mr Biggles's neck. If we find it, I'll prove he is a wizard," Feefeen whispered.

"If he catches us, I hope he doesn't turn us into frogs," Tawney giggled.

"He won't catch us. We will be in and out of here before you can say bubbly-squeak," Feefeen said.

They stepped into the hall and slowly opened a bedroom door. The night-light was on but Mr Biggles wasn't there.

"Tawney look, the amulet is on the table," Feefeen said. "I told you it would be easy. Now let's grab it before anyone wakes up."

"But that's stealing!" Toonie said.

"It's borrowing Toonie. We'll give it back to Mr Biggles tomorrow," Feefeen said.

He picked up the amulet but suddenly it started to glow. The amulet lit up the whole room.

"I am the property of Bertholomew Biggles. Not a toy for nosey, young bears. Release me or pay the price," it said.

"We are only borrowing you for a night. I'm sure your master won't mind," Feefeen grinned, shoving it in his pocket. "I told you he was a wizard!"

They hurried into the hall but Tawney tripped over a mop and bucket.

CRASH!

It fell over with a bang. A light came on at the other end of the hall.

"Quick run, we've woken up Mr Biggles," Feefeen whispered.

Toonie helped Tawney to his feet and they ran into their classroom. Glum, Mr Biggles' cat was in the way, hissing at them. The three cubs ran at him

and the cat jumped back with a yowl.

They jumped out the window and ran into the woods.

Feefeen looked back and saw Mr Biggles open the front door. The cubs hid behind some trees and kept very quiet.

"I hope he doesn't catch us," Feefeen muttered.

"Glum who entered the school?" they heard Mr Biggles ask.

"Three young, curious bears, Master. And they took your amulet," Glum hissed.

"Well, well... we may have to teach them a lesson," Mr Biggles said angrily.

"What did Mr Biggles mean 'teach them a lesson'?" Tawney asked.

"Shhh!" Toonie whispered, as they started to creep home.

"I don't know," Feefeen said. "But don't worry. He'll forget all about it after we give him back the amulet. See you in the morning!"

The following morning, Feefeen woke up early. He was excited. The amulet was hanging around his neck. Suddenly he heard a squeaky voice.

"Good morning, are you my master?" the voice asked.

Feefeen looked around the room. There was nobody there.

"Are you my master?" the voice asked again.

Feefeen spotted a little mouse. The mouse stared back. Then it spoke.

"Are you my master?"

"Who are you?" Feefeen asked.

"My name is Lenny Longtail. The owner of the amulet is my master," Lenny squeaked.

"But I don't want to be your master."

"The owner of the amulet is always my master. I must do as he orders. It is normally a powerful wizard. Are you a wizard? What happened to Bartholomew Biggles?"

"I borrowed it from him. Would you mind hiding in the wardrobe for a while?" Feefeen asked.

"I always do as my master wishes," Lenny said.

He flew across the room and landed in Feefeen's sock drawer.

Feefeen dressed and ran over to tell Toonie and Tawney. He burst into their kitchen but Mrs. Mac Tavish was there.

"Hi Feefeen, you're up early," she smiled.

"Good morning Mrs MacTavish!" Feefeen said. "Can Tawney and Toonie come over to my house after breakfast? I need to show them something."

"You and your secrets! They can go over in ten minutes Feefeen."

Feefeen ran home. He charged into his bedroom and opened the wardrobe. Lenny was still there.

"Lenny my friends have never met a mouse that can fly before so please don't do any magic unless I ask you to," Feefeen said.

"I will do as my master orders," Lenny squeaked.

Feefeen soon heard Toonie and Tawney running

up the stairs.

"What is the big secret Feefeen?" Toonie asked.

"Mam was surprised we didn't finish our breakfasts," Tawney added.

"Sit on the bed. Wait until you see this!" Feefeen grinned.

He opened his wardrobe.

Toonie and Tawney stared at the mouse.

"Lenny, these are my best friends, Toonie and Tawney," Feefeen said. "Say hello."

"Good morning young bears," Lenny said.

"A talking mouse!" Toonie and Tawney gulped.

"Now Lenny, please fly across the room and land on my bed."

Lenny floated across the room and landed on Feefeen's pillow.

Toonie and Tawney clapped.

"It's amazing – you can do magic," Toonie said.

"It's the amulet. And this is just the beginning," Feefeen said.

"Feefeen, Mr Biggles is a very powerful wizard and I'm sure he will want his amulet back," Tawney said.

"We will put it back tonight, after we've had some fun with it. Now what do you think of Lenny?" Feefeen asked.

"I have never met a flying mouse before," Toonie said.

"I am a magical mouse with special powers," Lenny Longtail said.

"What special powers do you have?" Tawney

asked.

"I have many powers. I can bring things to life."

"Will you show us?" Feefeen asked.

Lenny looked at Feefeen's slippers. He muttered a magical spell. Suddenly the slippers began to walk around the bedroom. The cubs laughed as the slippers began to dance. Then Lenny muttered another spell and the slippers stopped moving.

"Lenny, you will have to hide in my pocket for a while. Is that okay?" Feefeen asked.

"As my master commands," Lenny squeaked. He flew into Feefeen's pocket.

"I want to find out what else the amulet can do," Feefeen grinned.

"You're right," Toonie and Tawney said.

They went downstairs. Dolleen was standing at the front door with the shopping bag. "Do you want to come to the shop with me?" she asked.

"No thanks Dolleen, we're going to go for a walk in the woods," Feefeen said.

"Did you tell Mameen where you were going?" Dolleen frowned. "I hope you're not going to do anything stupid."

"I'm going to tell her now," Feefeen growled. "Don't be so bossy!"

Dolleen just waved and went off to the shops.

When she got there she bumped into Mr Biggles.

"Good morning Dolleen, is Feefeen with you?" he asked.

"No Mr Biggles, he's gone for a walk in the woods," she said.

"Oh well maybe you can help me Dolleen. Last night somebody came into our school and took something valuable belonging to me. I hope that they just borrowed it and they are planning to return it later. Do you know anything about it?" Mr Biggles asked.

Dolleen went red. Feefeen was such a pest.

"Uumm I don't know," Dolleen blushed. "I will run home and ask Feefeen if he knows anything about it."

"Thank you Dolleen. I'll be waiting at the school."

Meanwhile Feefeen, Toonie and Tawney were walking in the woods. They saw some rocks and sat down.

Feefeen put Lenny Longtail on top of one of the rocks.

"Lenny, what is the most powerful creature you have ever seen?" Feefeen asked.

"The most powerful of all creatures would have to be the White Dragon. Yes indeed, the White Dragon. He is powerful and cunning."

"And when did you meet him?" Feefeen asked.

"It was nearly 200 years ago. It was when my old master, Mr Biggles, fought the Dragon in the Silver Wars," Lenny said.

"Could we see a picture of the dragon?" Toonie asked.

"I can do better than that, I can summon him," Lenny said.

"Yes, ask him to come here!" Feefeen shouted. He jumped up with excitement. "I've always wanted to see a dragon."

Suddenly the amulet shone very brightly. A white mist came out of it.

The young bears were very surprised.

Then the mist started to grow and grow. It was all around them. They could see a dragon growing in the mist. He was huge, with long, white wings.

The mist blew away and they could see the White Dragon. He was asleep. He seemed to be under a spell.

"Lenny! He's beautiful but quick put him back!" Feefeen shouted.

The three bears were shaking with fright.

"I may summon him master, but only the master of the amulet can command the White Dragon to return to his resting place," Lenny squeaked.

"But Lenny, I don't know how to do that," Feefeen gasped.

"But you are the master of the amulet."

"No, I'm not. My friends and I borrowed the amulet from Mr Biggles," Feefeen muttered.

"Well you need to find him quickly. The Dragon is still asleep. He will wake up soon and he will be very, very hungry," Lenny whispered.

"And what does the White Dragon normally eat?" Tawney asked.

"Everything, especially young bears."

"I think we need to find Mr Biggles," Toonie said.

Feefeen grabbed Lenny and they ran off.

CRASH!

The three cubs had bumped into Dolleen.

"Feefeen, there you are! I just met Master Biggles

in the shop. He was asking about an amulet. Did you take it?"

"Dolleen, I'm in trouble. I did take it. I used it to summon a fierce dragon. And if I don't find Mr Biggles, we will all be eaten," Feefeen panted.

He was so scared he was still shaking.

"Feefeen, there are no such things as dragons. They are fairytales to frighten cubs," Dolleen snapped. She was sick of her brother's stories.

Suddenly, Lenny's head popped out of Feefeen's pocket

"The White Dragon is over real," he said.

"A TALKING MOUSE!" Dolleen shouted.

"Yes Lenny is a mouse that speaks and there is a dragon on the other side of Blacksmoke Mountain. And if we don't find Mr Biggles, we'll all be eaten!" Tawney wailed.

"Well Mr Biggles is at the school waiting for you to bring back his amulet," Dolleen said.

"Come on then!" Toonie said.

The four bears ran to the school. They found Mr Biggles in the classroom.

"Mr Biggles, Mr Biggles. We need your help," Dolleen panted. She quickly told him what had happened.

"Feefeen, give me the amulet. We may still have time to return the White Dragon to the Land of Sleep," Mr Biggles said.

Feefeen gave it to him and they all rushed back to the woods.

They were just in time. The White Dragon was beginning to wake up.

"Wizard Biggles your sleep spell is starting to wear off. Soon I will be able to move and I will eat you and your friends," it hissed.

"No you won't!" Mr Biggles said. "I will send you back to the Land of Sleep for another 200 years!"

"You won't have time and I am very, very hungry. Look, now I can move my wing."

"You are the fiercest creature in the universe but you will not hurt any of us," Mr Biggles growled.

"I will kill you with my flame," the White Dragon said, as flames suddenly spouted from its nose.

The four, young bears hid behind the Wizard.

"Oh no you won't!" Mr Biggles shouted.

He waved his hands and cast a spell. Suddenly blue mist appeared and the dragon started to melt away.

"Nooooo!" it shouted, as it was sucked back into the amulet.

Feefeen could see a flame inside the amulet. Then it went out.

The four bear cubs were shaking.

"I think we need to have a word Feefeen," Mr Biggles growled. He was very angry. They could all have been killed.

"It wasn't my fault. It was the mouse," Feefeen cried.

"Don't try and blame Lenny. You know you should never take anything without asking. This is what happens when you steal things," Mr Biggles growled.

"I am very sorry for stealing it and nearly waking the White Dragon up," Feefeen said.

"We are very, very sorry too!" Tawney and Toonie said.

"Well let it be a lesson to you and in future. Listen to Dolleen! She'll help you stay out of trouble. Now I want you three to clean up the classroom for me and mop the floors for the rest of the week," Mr Biggles said.

"Yes Mr Biggles," they said.

"Master," Lenny Longtail said.

"Yes Lenny?" Mr Biggles smiled.

"May I stay here and have a holiday with Feefeen and his friends?" he asked.

"Yes you can Lenny and while you're here try to get him to learn an important lesson....

"What Mr Biggles?" they all asked, waiting for him to finish.

"Let Sleeping Dragons Lie!"

Feefeen
and the Haunted House

It was a bright, summer morning when Feefeen woke up. He jumped out of bed and got dressed in his camping clothes. He rushed downstairs and into the kitchen.

"Hi Mameen," Feefeen smiled.

"Good Morning, Feefeen. Would you like honey on your pancakes?" Mameen asked.

"I would love some please. Is Dolleen ready yet?"

"I am indeed," Dolleen grinned, walking in.

"Do you have the tent?" he asked.

"It is in my rucksack," Dolleen replied.

"I love camping!" he laughed.

There was a knock on the front door. Mameen opened it. Tawney and Toonie were standing there, with ear-to-ear smiles on their faces.

"Good Morning Mrs MacRageen, is Feefeen ready?" Toonie asked.

Mameen turned around to call Feefeen but he was already standing right behind her.

"Yes Toonie, Feefeen's ready!" she laughed. "Now remember cubs, no speaking to strangers and make sure you are all back here no later than lunch-time tomorrow – and Dolleen you are in charge."

"This is going to be a wonderful adventure," Feefeen smiled.

Mameen waved them off.

They walked over the hill towards Farmer Crank's orchard.

"Feefeen are you sure Farmer Crank gave us permission to camp in his field?" Dolleen asked.

"After what happened with his salmon I'm surprised he said yes."

"I don't think he'd mind," Feefeen said in a small voice.

"Feefeen, you said you had asked him. I told Mameen you had - did you ask Farmer Crank or not?" Dolleen asked.

"Well not exactly, Dolleen."

"Feefeen MacRageen, you are a little deeevil!"

"I suppose he won't mind for one night," Dolleen groaned.

They turned a corner and saw an orchard full of apple and pear trees.

"Isn't it lovely?" Feefeen said.

The four bears picked up apples from the ground and ate them.

"Yum, yum these apples are tasty," Tawney said.

"I love crunchy apples!" Toonie added.

"We need to find a large tree. We'll put the tent under it in case it rains," Dolleen said.

"What about that old, oak tree over there?" Toonie pointed.

"That's a wonderful spot Toonie. Now Feefeen, you help me set up the tent. Toonie, Tawney will you collect some firewood? Camping wouldn't be camping without a fire," Dolleen smiled.

"We'll be back in few minutes, Dolleen," Tawney said.

"Okay! Feefeen, we need to find all the tent pegs," Dolleen said.

"One, two, three, four, five, six – Dolleen, I have

six pegs. I thought there were only four corners on a tent?" Feefeen asked.

"That's true Feefeen, but we need six pegs, four for the corners and two for the front of the tent."

They opened up the tent and stretched it out on the ground. Dolleen placed two poles inside the tent and Feefeen gave her a rod to put across the top.

"Feefeen, these are called support bars. They hold the tent up," Dolleen said. "Now you need to hammer in the pegs."

She looked over at Feefeen. He was fast asleep on the ground!

In the woods, Toonie and Tawney were munching apples and collecting firewood. They came upon a giant hedge. The two bears pushed their way through it. There was an old mansion on the other side of the hedge.

"I wonder who lives in that house," Toonie said.

"Let's find out," Tawney grinned.

They walked over to the house and hopped onto the porch. It creaked loudly.

"Let's go inside," Tawney said.

The two bears tip-toed into the house.

"Look at all the cobwebs and dust," Toonie whispered. "It's creepy.

"Ha, ha Toonie – those pictures are full of angry faces. They look funny."

"Tawney, I'm scared. I want to go back to Dolleen."

"Don't be such a coward Toonie... let's investi-

gate," he grinned.
"I have a bad feeling Tawney…"

Suddenly, a voice yelled:

"HE HAS A BAD FEELING ABOUT OUR HOUSE – ISN'T HE A CLEVER BEAR? PERHAPS WE SHOULD EAT HIM SECOND!"

"Ahhh!" Toonie shouted.
"What was that?" Tawney yelled, at the same time. They flew out of the house.

In the orchard, Dolleen finally had the tent set up. As she stood back to admire it, Toonie and Tawney rushed out of the trees and crashed into the tent, flattening it.

Dolleen was very cross.

"And what do you pair think you are doing? It took me half an hour to fix that tent while Feefeen slept like a pillow," Dolleen shouted angrily.

"… … … a … . g h … . g h h … … … g h o s t … … . a ghost……." Toonie mumbled.

"Tawney what is your brother babbling about?" Dolleen asked.

"A scary voice said it was going to eat us," Tawney said.

"We saw a ghost Dolleen," Toonie shivered. "We heard its horrible voice."

"There are no such things as ghosts Toonie and who ever heard of a ghost living in an apple orchard?

You're not making sense," Dolleen answered.

"A real ghost, yippee. I've always wanted to see a ghost," Feefeen said.

All the noise had woken him up.

"Feefeen there are no such thing as ghosts," Dolleen said.

"Yes there are," Toonie and Tawney shouted.

"Where?" Dolleen asked.

"On the other side of the giant hedge there is a haunted house," Toonie shivered.

"I want to see! I want to see!" Feefeen said, starting to run off.

"Feefeen MacRageen, hold your horses – if we are going to investigate this we are going to do it together. Toonie, Tawney, lead the way," Dolleen ordered.

"I am not gooooing back there. That voice was creepy and I'm scared," Toonie said.

"I don't mind going back. It was only a silly old voice," Tawney said.

"I want to see the ghost's face," Feefeen grinned.

"I am not going back there," Toonie groaned.

"Toonie we are going to stick together so you don't have to worry," Feefeen replied.

"Feefeen none of us are going unless we all go. Now Toonie there are no such thing as ghosts. Come back to the house and I'll show you I'm right," Dolleen replied.

"Come on Toonie, just come with us. We mightn't even see the ghost," Feefeen said. "Don't be so scared!"

"Feefeen there is no ghost and that's the end of it,"

Dolleen said.

Toonie was still shaking. He didn't want to go back to the house but he didn't want to be left on his own either.

"Don't worry I'll take care of you. I'm not afraid of any old ghost," Dolleen smiled.

"Come on Toonie," Tawney said.

"Okay, I'll come with you," Toonie mumbled.

The four bears pushed through the huge hedge. Feefeen gasped when he saw the spooky old mansion.

"Look, it's a real haunted house," he said.

He ran onto the porch and pushed open the front door.

"Is everyone shivering?" Feefeen laughed loudly, stepping inside.

"Feefeen be careful," Dolleen said, as they followed him into the house.

"Toonie, where is the ghost?" Feefeen asked.

"We didn't actually see him. He spoke to us from up there," Tawney pointed.

"He said he was going to eat us," Toonie groaned.

Feefeen tip-toed over to the stairs.

"Hey don't go up there," Dolleen said.

Feefeen laughed and ran upstairs.

"There's nothing up here," he grinned.

Suddenly, a ghost appeared behind him.

Dolleen, Tawney and Toonie stared at the ghost, glued to the spot.

"What's wrong with all of you?" Feefeen asked.

"WOOOOOHHHH. I'M GOING TO EAT YOU UP LITTLE BEAR," the ghost wailed.

Feefeen spun around and shouted with fright.

"Ahhhhh! Dolleen help!"

"WHO SAID YOU COULD COME INTO MY HOUSE?"

Feefeen gulped.

"Ooooh let's get out of here," Toonie and Tawney shouted.

They flew out the front door but Dolleen bravely climbed up the stairs.

"You leave my brother alone, you big bully," she said.

"LEAVE MY HOUSE IMMEDIATELY!"

Dolleen grabbed Feefeen's arm and they rushed out the door.

It slammed behind them.

Feefeen and Dolleen ran to the trees. Toonie and Tawney were hiding in the hedge.

"I told you!" Toonie said. He was still shaking.

"We have to go back," Feefeen whispered.

"Are you mad Feefeen? The ghost will eat us," Toonie whispered.

"I don't believe we just saw a ghost," Dolleen said. "It must have been somebody pretending to be a ghost."

"No way Dolleen, it was a ghost," Feefeen said.

"I don't believe in ghosts," she said.

"Well let's go back and see if it really was a ghost. Then we can find out if it is a friendly or an unfriendly one," Feefeen said.

"I want to go home," Toonie said.

"Toonie, we are not going home. We are four brave bears and we are going to talk to that ghost," Feefeen said. "I bet he's friendly."

"But he said he wants to eat us," Tawney said.

"Why would a ghost want to eat us Tawney? Anyway we're not afraid of an old ghost!" Feefeen said.

"I am," Toonie mumbled.

"No you are not Toonie MacTavish! You are going to come back into that house with me and talk to the ghost!" Feefeen said.

Toonie and Tawney looked at Dolleen.

"Okay, let's go back and find out who's playing a joke on us," she said.

They crept back towards the house. Feefeen gently pushed the door open. It was very quiet.

"Come on," he urged.

Dolleen was right behind him.

"This is a very frightening house," Toonie said.

"It has frightened the life out of me," Tawney replied.

"Come here, brave little bears," a quiet voice said.

Feefeen looked around. It wasn't coming from upstairs.

"Over here," the voice said.

Feefeen looked at an ornament on the fireplace. It was of an old man and an old woman, standing together. The old man was banging his stick: Tuck! Tuck! Tuck!

"Ahhh!" Toonie and Tawney screamed.

"It's coming from that ornament," Dolleen said.

"It must be a recording."

They walked over to have a look.

"Yes, yes, it's us. Come here brave, little bears," the old woman in the ornament said. "It is wonderful to have someone to talk to again. Who are you?"

"My name is Feefeen MacRageen. This is my sister Dolleen and these are my best friends, Toonie and Tawney MacTavish," Feefeen answered. "Who are you?"

Toonie and Tawney were too scared to say anything. Dolleen was looking around to see if someone was hiding in the room. She was sure it was all a joke. There was no way an ornament could talk!

"My name is Azrael and this is my husband Camelon. Our son Askan is upstairs. I think he frightened you but he was only joking," Azrael said.

"See I told you they were friendly ghosts," Feefeen said to Toonie. "Were you always ornaments?"

"No, no, of course not – we were once bears like you. The pictures on the walls are pictures of our family. Many years ago a wicked witch placed a curse on us. She made us ghosts who had to live in this ornament. The witch also made our son Askan a ghost. He is a prisoner in the top half of the house," Camelon said.

"See Dolleen – I told you ghosts are real!" Feefeen grinned.

"Oh my, oh my," Dolleen said.

She looked a bit scared. There was no-one hiding in the house. They really were ghosts.

"Why would a witch curse poor, innocent bears?"

she asked.

"She was a very cruel witch who my family caught 300 years ago. They were going to send her to prison but she was very powerful. She escaped and cast a spell on us. We have been prisoners in this house ever since," Azrael said.

"300 years! That is dreadful, Azrael. How do you break the curse?" Feefeen asked.

"There is only one way. A brave warrior must sleep one full night in our house. Then we will vanish and be at peace," Azrael said.

"I am a brave warrior. I'll spend the night here and release you from the witch's curse," Feefeen said.

"No, Feefeen don't do it!" Tawney and Toonie shouted.

They were still afraid of the ghosts.

"You are a very brave bear," Azrael said.

Feefeen looked pleased.

"I don't know Feefeen. Mameen said I was in charge and she will be very cross if anything happens to you," Dolleen said. "Azrael, can we all spend the night?"

"No Dolleen, it has to be just one brave warrior on his own. It's the only way to break the curse."

"Feefeen, are you sure you want to do this?" Dolleen asked.

"Dolleen I have to help them. Please let me," he said.

"Okay Feefeen. If you are frightened we will be camping just outside. If anything happens, just call out and we will come straight in. Isn't that right?"

Dolleen said to Toonie and Tawney.

Toonie nodded but Tawney was busy gazing at the gold ring on the old woman's finger.

"We will go and collect the tent from Farmer Crank's orchard. Maybe you should come with us and we can all come back together," Dolleen said.

She was worried about leaving Feefeen behind.

"Dolleen, I'll be fine. I'm sure Azrael and Camelon will take good care of me," Feefeen smiled.

Dolleen, Toonie and Tawney walked back to the tent.

"Dolleen, did you believe her story?" Tawney asked.

"I'm not sure Tawney. I didn't think ghosts were real and now we're mixed up with ghosts and magic. I don't like it. It would be better if we all stayed in the house, not just Feefeen. The sooner we set up camp outside that old house, the happier I'll be," Dolleen muttered.

In the old mansion, Feefeen walked along the halls looking at the pictures. Some of them were scary. One woman looked just like Azrael. She had a long witch-like cloak. She looked very wicked.

Feefeen shivered. Now that the other three bears had left he was scared. He stared at the picture and started to shake. It had to be Azrael. She had lied to him. She was the witch.

"HA, HA. STUPID, LITTLE BEAR. WE'VE CAUGHT YOU IN OUR TRAP," the ghost upstairs shouted.

Feefeen gulped. He knew he was in big trouble. He made a dash for the front door. But it was locked.

"Brave, little Feefeen wants to leave our house but we couldn't allow that," Azrael whispered.

"Not when we need him to get us out of this prison. His curiosity has got him into deep trouble," Camelon snarled.

Feefeen tried to open the door again but it didn't budge.

"I tried to help you. Why are you doing this to me, you horrible things?" he pleaded.

"You are a silly bear. You should have listened to your sister," Azrael said.

"Dolleen! Help. Dolleen, Dolleen," Feefeen shouted.

"She can't help you now Feefeen. You will soon fall asleep and when morning comes you won't wake up. Then we will be free," Azrael said.

"You are an evil creature Azrael. Dolleen will rescue me. She will not let you harm me," Feefeen roared.

He was starting to feel sleepy.

"She doesn't know our secret. She can't help you," Azrael snarled.

Suddenly, Feefeen was so dizzy he couldn't stand up any more. He slumped to the ground and fell fast asleep.

"Ha, ha, ha!" the ghosts laughed.

It was dark when Dolleen, Toonie and Tawney got

back to the old mansion.

'Toonie, will you and Tawney collect firewood? I'll put the tent up again," Dolleen said.

Toonie and Tawney came back with firewood just as Dolleen finished with the tent. They built a fire.

"Let's roast some apples," Toonie said.

"I love roast apple," Dolleen said. "Feefeen will be sorry he's staying with Azrael and missing this."

"Did you see that ring on her hand?" Toonie asked.

"Of course I did. I was surprised. It was the same ring that witch-woman was wearing in the picture," Dolleen said.

"Why would Azrael want the witch's ring?" Tawney asked.

Dolleen suddenly jumped up.

"Toonie, you're a genius. Azrael is the witch. It is her ring. That is why she wears it. I should have guessed earlier. And now they have Feefeen but not for long," Dolleen yelled.

She ran towards the house.

Toonie and Tawney rushed after her.

"I'll save you Feefeen," Dolleen shouted.

The three bears burst through the front door.

Azrael was chanting spells.

"You nasty witch, where is my brother?" Dolleen shouted.

"You are too late. Your brother is in a deep, deep, sleep," she laughed.

"I know how to wake him up," Dolleen yelled.

Suddenly she ran to the fireplace and picked up the ornament.

"NO, put us down you fool," Camelon growled.

"Get away from us," Azrael shouted.

"If I break this ornament you won't be able to hurt Feefeen," Dolleen yelled.

Toonie and Tawney quickly lifted Feefeen up and carried him outside.

CRASH!

Dolleen had dropped the ornament.

"Noooooo!" Azrael and Cameron screamed, as they smashed into little pieces.

"Ahhhhhhh!" Askan yelled.

Dolleen had broken the curse and the ghosts were gone.

"That's the end of those bad ghosts," she said.

She went outside and helped Feefeen to stand up.

"Dolleen, you found out that Azrael was the witch, didn't you?" he grinned at her.

"Those ghosts won't he haunting this house anymore!" Dolleen laughed.

"It's wonderful having such a clever sister," Feefeen said, smiling.

"Let's just forget about them!" Dolleen said.

"What's for supper?" Toonie asked.

"Don't you ever think of anything other than filling your tummies?" Dolleen grinned.

"NO!" Toonie, Tawney and Feefeen laughed.

Feefeen
and the Hot Air Balloon

Every year Feefeen visited his Aunt Meebeen and Uncle McDougal on his birthday.

Mameen came into his bedroom carrying a hot plate of pancakes. As a birthday treat they were covered in chocolate and honey.

"Happy Birthday, Feefeen! Remember, we will be leaving for Aunt Meebeen's at 11 o'clock," she said.

Feefeen looked at the plate.

"Birthday pancakes are a great start to the day!"

"Six-year-old bear cubs are always hungry," Mameen smiled.

Feefeen laughed and ate them all up.

"Yum!" he shouted. He licked his fingers.

"Come on. Up you get!" Mameen said.

She pulled him out of bed and gave him a birthday hug.

Feefeen got dressed. He heard a knock on the front door and ran downstairs.

He opened it and Toonie and Tawney MacTavish, his best friends were outside. They lived across the lane.

Tawney handed Feefeen a present.

"Happy Birthday, Feefeen," Tawney said.

"Happy birthday, Feefeen," Toonie grinned.

"Thank you, thank you!" Feefeen shouted.

"Are you going to visit your aunt in the countryside today?" Tawney asked.

"Yes... we're leaving soon," he said.

"Can we come?" Toonie asked.

"Oh that would be fun. I'll ask Mameen. Come in," Feefeen said.

They went into the sitting-room.

"Happy Birthday Feefeen," Dolleen grinned. "I'll give you your present later!"

"Thanks Dolleen," Feefeen smiled. "Mameen, can Toonie and Tawney come with us?"

"Oh, I'm sure that will be alright. Your Aunt Meebeen loves cubs visiting. I'll pop over and ask your parents for you," Mameen said.

Feefeen opened his presents.

"Mmmmm! Two big jars of honey! Thank you!" Feefeen grinned. "Look, Mameen is coming back. I hope you can come."

"That's fine cubs – you can come with us," Mameen said.

"Oooh yippee, yippee, Toonie and Tawney are coming," Feefeen said, jumping up and down.

"Hip, hip hurray!" Tawney and Toonie laughed, dancing about.

Dolleen laughed too because they looked so silly.

"Feefeen, we need to leave in the next five minutes. Go and get ready. Your Aunt Meebeen doesn't like it when people are late," Mameen said.

"Everyone into the car," Mameen shouted.

Dolleen sat beside Mameen in the front seat and Feefeen got into the back.

"Why do I always get the back seat? It's not fair and it's my birthday," Feefeen complained.

"Maybe it's because you are always last out Feefeen. Anyway Toonie and Tawney will be sharing it with you," Dolleen said.

Feefeen's two best friends jumped into the seat beside him and grinned.

Mameen started the car and they were on their way.

About an hour later, they arrived outside Aunt Meebeen's gates. She lived in a big house in the countryside.

"Well children, we are finally here," Mameen said. "Dolleen, please open the gates."

"Okay," Dolleen smiled.

"Mameen, is Aunt Meebeen very rich?" Feefeen asked.

"Yes, I suppose you could say she is rich, but she is very generous. Dolleen jump in and let's not keep Meebeen waiting any longer," Mameen said.

They drove up the tree-lined avenue, to an enormous, red-brick mansion.

"Wow, your Aunt Meebeen has a huge house, Feefeen," Toonie mumbled.

They stopped at the front door. It flew open and Meebeen, Mameen's eldest sister, came out. She was wearing an apron and a straw hat. She rushed over to her sister and gave her a hug. She lifted Dolleen and kissed her on the forehead. Finally, she looked at Feefeen. He blushed.

"Who's six years old today?" Meebeen asked.

She took a present out of her apron and handed it to him.

"Thank you Aunt Meebeen," Feefeen said.

"We'll put it in the car and he can open it later,"

Mameen said.

Aunt Meebeen looked at Toonie and Tawney

"And who do we have here?" she asked.

"Toonie and Tawney MacTavish. They are Feefeen's best friends in Salmonswood," Mameen answered.

"Hello cubs, it is wonderful to see you," Meebeen said. "There are lemonade and fresh honey cakes on the table inside."

"Yippee," Feefeen shouted. "I love honey cakes!"

The four cubs flew into the house.

Mameen and Meebeen smiled and followed them inside.

"Where is MacDougal?" Mameen asked.

"In the north field – the old fool thinks of nothing but flying. He has built a hot air balloon and spends his afternoons flying around in it. I'm sure he will have an accident one of these days," Aunt Meebeen said. "Bears were not designed to fly. If we were meant to fly we would have wings!"

"Now Meebeen, your husband is a very clever bear. I am sure this is just another hobby like all the others. He will get tired of it soon," Mameen said.

"I hope so," Meebeen groaned.

They found the four bear cubs munching honey cakes and drinking lemonade.

"Aunt Meebeen, where is Uncle McDougal?" Dolleen asked.

"He is in his workshop with his new hot air balloon," Aunt Meebeen answered.

"A hot air balloon – what's that?" Feefeen asked.

"It's a huge balloon, with a basket under it. Your uncle climbs into the basket and fills the balloon full of air. Then he can fly around for a few minutes or until it crashes," Aunt Meebeen sighed.

"Oooh heee hee, a hot air balloon," Feefeen grinned. "Mameen, I want to see it! May we go and visit Uncle McDougal's workshop?"

"Of course, but be very careful in the north field. Dolleen don't let them go near that deep pond," Mameen said.

"Ok Mameen," Dolleen said. "Don't worry."

They started walking to the workshop. Toonie spotted an old shed.

"I wonder what that shed is used for," Toonie asked.

"It could be haunted," Tawney said.

"Haunted! Don't be silly Tawney. Why would an old shed be haunted?" Dolleen asked.

"I'm not going near that shed," Tawney whispered.

"Are you afraid Tawney?" Feefeen laughed.

Suddenly a fully-dressed rooster and his wife stepped out of the shed.

The four bear cubs jumped back. They were very surprised.

"What are you doing here?" Mrs Loudcry yelled. She had got a fright too. "Who are you and why are you staring at our house?"

"Yes why are you here? You don't live here. Well answer me," Mr Loudcry said.

Dolleen started giggling. Toonie and Tawney

looked a little scared.

Feefeen grinned and stepped forward.

"Good morning, sir. I am sorry if we scared you or your wife but we are allowed to be here. We are visiting our Aunt Meebeen who owns the big house," Feefeen said.

"Your apology is accepted," Mr Loudcry replied.

Each bear gently shook his wing to show that they were now friends.

"My name is Rooster Loudcry. This is my wife Mildred Loudcry. Well it was a pleasure meeting you, but my wife and I are very busy," Rooster said. "Goodbye."

The bears waved as Rooster and Mildred went back into the shed.

The four bears walked to the pond.

"Don't go too near it!" Dolleen said.

"Sshhhh!" Feefeen said. He pointed at a frog and a swan. They were talking. Mr Frog was in fits of laughter. His wobbly tummy shook as he laughed.

"I heard that old fool McDougal has built a balloon that can fly," Mr Frog said.

"McDougal has lost his mind. Who ever heard of bears flying? I'm not too fond of flying myself," the Swan said.

She noticed the cubs.

"Good morning to you all," she said.

"Are you lost?" Mr Frog asked.

"We are visiting our Aunt Meebeen and Uncle

McDougal and we are looking for his workshop," Dolleen answered.

"Workshop? Oh you mean his old shed... it's around the corner," Ms Swan laughed.

The bears thanked them and walked on.

They arrived at a large shed. Feefeen saw Uncle McDougal working at the back, on a big piece of machinery.

"Uncle McDougal it's me, Feefeen," Feefeen yelled.

"Uncle McDougal, it's Dolleen. We've come to visit," she shouted.

McDougal looked up and smiled.

"Hello Dolleen. Happy Birthday Feefeen! And who do we have here?" he asked.

Dolleen introduced Toonie and Tawney.

Uncle McDougal shook paws with them.

"They are Feefeen's best friends in Salmonswood," Dolleen said.

"Aunt Meebeen told us you built a hot air balloon, Uncle McDougal – is it true?" Feefeen asked. He was jumping up and down with excitement.

"Yes and it flies. I am giving it another test run this afternoon. As it's your birthday Feefeen, you can all come with me if you want, but you have to ask your mother first," McDougal said.

"Yes, please!" Feefeen said. "Where will we sit?"

"We can't sit down Feefeen. We'll have to stand in that basket instead. When the balloon is full of air it's able to carry us but only for a short while,"

McDougal said. "Do you see the levers, the things sticking out of this box? They pump air into the balloon. And this rope makes the balloon stay on the ground. When I untie the rope the balloon flies away."

"It is amazing, Uncle McDougal," Feefeen said.

"I have to get some tools out of the house now cubs. Dolleen, will you come and help me?" Mc Dougal asked.

"Ok Uncle McDougal," Dolleen smiled.

"The three of you wait here," McDougal said, as they walked off.

"I wonder if your Uncle would mind if we had a look?" Tawney asked.

Feefeen climbed into the balloon basket.

"I'm sure he wouldn't mind," he said.

Toonie and Tawney climbed in beside him.

Feefeen started messing. He turned one of the levers and hot air blew into the balloon. He turned it off and grinned.

Toonie looked at Feefeen and turned the lever again.

More hot air went into the balloon. The balloon was filling up.

Toonie turned the lever all the way and hot air flew into the balloon.

The three bears laughed.

"This is a wonderful birthday adventure. Hurray" Feefeen shouted.

The balloon was almost full. Feefeen looked at his friends.

"Imagine if we untied that rope. We could fly into

the sky," he said.

"We will get into serious trouble," Toonie said and laughed.

They all wanted to fly the balloon by themselves.

"It's my birthday," Feefeen grinned, "I can't wait until this afternoon and Mameen might say no. Will I untie the rope?"

"Yes!" Tawney and Toonie shouted.

Feefeen climbed out of the basket and ran over to the rope. He untied it and climbed back in again.

The balloon slowly started to rise up and the three bears cheered.

"Hurray! Hurray! We're flying," they shouted.

Dolleen was on her way back to the house when she heard them.

"Uncle McDougal!" she shouted.

She pointed at the hot air balloon

"Oh no... my balloon must have come loose!" he said.

"Look, Feefeen, Toonie and Tawney are in the basket under the balloon," Dolleen said..

McDougal was very upset.

"Why did I leave them on their own? I should have known the temptation would be too much. Feefeen is just like his father. He always finds mischief," Uncle McDougal said. "Quick we'll run to the garage and follow them in the car. They won't go too far."

Feefeen, Toonie and Tawney were smiling in the balloon

"Hurray we're flying!" Toonie said.

"This is the best birthday I've ever had," Feefeen shouted.

Feefeen looked over the side of the basket and saw Dolleen and Uncle McDougal running to the house. He waved at them.

McDougal and Dolleen ran into the kitchen where Mameen and Aunt Meebeen were drinking tea.

"Feefeen and his friends have taken my balloon and are flying across the countryside," McDougal shouted. "We might be able to catch them in the car."

Mameen and Meebeen jumped up.

"If anything happens to those children I will never forgive you McDougal," Meebeen said.

"Neither will I," Mameen said.

They all got into the car.

"Look, they're over there," Dolleen said.

"Can this car go any faster?" Mameen begged.

They raced after the balloon.

Dolleen looked up at the balloon and watched as it started to fall.

"The balloon must have run out of gas. It's losing height," McDougal said.

"Did you show them how to land?" Aunt Meebeen asked.

"I never got the chance to show them anything. I was going to bring them all for a balloon ride this afternoon for Feefeen's birthday," McDougal answered.

"Oh no, I hope there isn't a terrible accident," Aunt Meeben said.

Mameen's face went white she was so worried.

The car flew along, chasing the balloon. It looked

like it was drifting back to the house.

"Can we go higher?" Toonie asked.
"Let's find out," Tawney answered. He pulled a lever but nothing happened. There was no more hot air.
"Feefeen the balloon isn't full of air any more," Tawney said.
Toonie pulled a different lever but tThe balloon kept falling down towards the ground.
Tawney pulled the lever again. There was no air left.
"What will we do?" Tawney asked.
"I don't know," Feefeen answered. He was scared. "Maybe if we land in an open field, we will be okay."
"I can't see any open fields around here," Tawney answered.
The three bears looked over the edge of the basket and searched for a big field.
They saw Aunt Meebeen's house.
"We're nearly at the north field. Maybe it will land there," Toonie yelled.
The balloon kept falling.

In the north field Mr Loudcry and his wife were sitting at their table. He was eating a large kernel of corn and his wife was knitting.
"Weren't they four lovely bear cubs we met today?" Mr Loudcry said.
"Very respectable – I hope we see them again before they leave," Mrs Loudcry replied.
CRASH!

Suddenly there was a loud bang. The hot air balloon had landed on top of the Loudcrys' house.

The roof of the shed fell down on top of Mr and Mrs Loudcry. There was dust and broken furniture everywhere. When the air cleared, Feefeen's head peeped out of the basket.

"Phew that was very scary," Feefeen said.

"It was a wonderful adventure," Toonie said.

"Where are we?" Tawney asked.

"You landed on my house and you have destroyed it!" Mr Loudcry shouted.

Mrs Loudcry shook her feathers out, trying to get rid of some of the dust. Her face was as red as a tomato.

"I thought you were such polite bears," she said angrily.

Feefeen felt bad.

"I'm very sorry. It was an accident" he said.

"Accident! Accident! Three bear cubs in a balloon... that is no accident," Mrs Loudcry shouted. She was very cross.

Feefeen didn't know what to say. He saw The McDougals, Mameen and Dolleen arrive in the car. His Mameen and Dolleen rushed over, smiling with relief. They helped the three cubs climb out of the basket.

"Don't ever do anything that stupid again Feefeen!" Mameen said.

"Who is going to pay to have our home rebuilt?" Mrs Loudcry asked.

"Good morning Mr and Mrs Loudcry. I will pay of course. It's all my fault and I'm very sorry,"

McDougal said.

"You weren't in the balloon," Mr Loudcry said.

"Yes, but it was my hot air balloon that did the damage."

"That is very fair of you and we'd be glad to accept," Mrs Loudcry said.

"Please don't be too hard on the young 'uns. We were all young and foolish once," Mr Loudcry said.

"Now you three cubs, come here!" McDougal ordered.

Feefeen, Toonie and Tawney looked scared as they stood in front of McDougal. He looked very serious.

"You all have to promise you'll never do something like this again," McDougal said. "You could have been killed."

"We promise," they said.

"We are very sorry, Uncle McDougal. It was all a horrible accident," Feefeen said. "But it was the best birthday present ever!"

Feefeen
and the Dolphins

The sound of running water disturbed Mameen's dreams. As she woke up, she saw a light outside the bedroom door. Bumble was snoring beside her. He was the heaviest sleeper in Salmonswood.

Mameen looked at the clock. It was very late.

"I better go and find out what that's all about!" Mameen muttered.

She got out of bed and wrapped herself in her favourite jumper. She walked quietly to the bathroom and opened the door.

Feefeen was sitting beside the bath on a small stool. He was holding a fishing rod.

"Feefeen, why are you fishing at this hour?" Mameen asked.

"Mameen I am practising how to catch a fish, like Tawney did," he said.

"Feefeen it is very late. You should be fast asleep in bed," Mameen said.

"Tawney caught a fish and I want to catch one!"

"I will ask your father to bring you and Dolleen out fishing with your Uncle Brutumus tomorrow morning but now its time for bed Feefeen."

Feefeen was so excited he jumped up.

"Will Uncle Brutumus really bring us fishing on his boat? I have to go and tell Dolleen," he shouted.

"Ssshhh, Feefeen. Don't wake up your sister," Mameen said.

She bent down and lifted Feefeen up. She carried him back to bed and kissed him on the forehead.

"Sweet dreams," Mameen said, as she shut the door.

The following morning, Feefeen woke up early. He dressed and went down to breakfast. Bumble was making fishcakes. Dolleen was busy reading the local newspaper, 'The Salmonswood Gazette'.

"Well Feefeen, are you ready for your first boat trip?" Mameen asked. She had just hung up the phone. "Your Uncle Brutumus said he'll take you."

"Of course I am," Feefeen grinned and tucked into his fishcakes.

After breakfast, Bumble, Dolleen and Feefeen kissed Mameen goodbye and drove off.

They quickly reached the seaside town of Logswood. They stopped at their Uncle Brutumus's boat. He was waiting for them.

"Hello fisher-folk!" Uncle Brutumus smiled.

He tickled Dolleen and Feefeen and smiled at Bumble.

"Hi Brutumus," Bumble said.

"Good morning Bumble. It is a surprise to see you here. I thought Lavender was coming because you are afraid of the sea."

"She couldn't come so I said I'd bring them fishing instead," Bumble said.

"So cubs are you ready to go fishing?" Brutumus asked.

"Yes! I want to catch a fish, a big fish," Feefeen shouted.

"Have you ever been on a boat before?" Uncle Brutumus asked.

"No, never," Feefeen grinned.

"Neither have I Uncle Brutumus," Dolleen said.

"We'll have loads of fun. I have extra fishing rods for you on the boat. But first you have to put on some life-jackets, so all aboard," Uncle Brutumus said.

They had to walk across a plank to get onto the boat.

"Be careful walking on the plank. I don't want you to slip into the water. It's very, very deep," he said.

Feefeen and Dolleen tip-toed across the plank. They grinned at each other. It was exciting to be on a boat.

Uncle Brutumus smiled at the two young cubs. He was very happy they were all going fishing.

"Now listen up cubs. When we're out at sea you have to do exactly what I tell you to do. On the boat my name is Captain Brutumus and I'm the boss," he smiled.

"Aye, aye Captain," Dolleen and Feefeen shouted.

"Now put on these life-jackets and we'll set sail."

Bumble helped the cubs put them on.

Brutumus went to the steering wheel and started the boat. He steered it out towards the open sea.

"Feefeen, Dolleen come here and I will show you how to steer a boat," Captain Brutumus said.

Feefeen grabbed the wheel but it was too heavy. It spun in his hands.

"It's not as easy as it looks Feefeen is it?" Captain Brutumus laughed.

He helped Feefeen to straighten the boat.

Then Dolleen had a go. She was very good at

steering the boat.

"You have your grandfather's skill Dolleen," Captain Brutumus said.

"Thanks Captain," Dolleen grinned.

"Bumble, are the rods ready?" he asked.

Bumble carried the fishing rods over to Dolleen and Feefeen.

"Cubs your uncle will help you to cast a fishing line," Bumble said.

"Dad, why aren't you fishing?" Dolleen asked.

"I don't feel too well at the moment. The sea doesn't agree with my tummy. I'm sure your uncle will be delighted to help you," Bumble groaned.

"Captain Brutumus, will you help me?" Feefeen asked.

"Of course I will Feefeen," he replied.

Captain Brutumus held the rod and helped Feefeen throw his line out into the sea.

"Are you ready to fish Dolleen?" he asked.

"No Captain! I'll steer the boat if that's ok?"

"That's fine Dolleen! Bumble, would you like to lie down inside my cabin for a few minutes?" Brutumus asked.

"A wonderful idea," Bumble groaned and went into the cabin.

Suddenly, Feefeen let out a happy scream.

"I've got one, got one; I've got a bite."

"Feefeen, don't pull the line in too quickly. If you do the fish will get away," Captain Brutumus said.

Feefeen gently wound the line in. The fish on the line was jumping around a lot. It didn't want to be caught.

"Dolleen, shut off the engine and hold the steering wheel," Captain Brutumus said.

"Aye, aye Captain!"

The boat stopped.

Feefeen kept winding up the fishing line. Suddenly an old Wellington boot popped out of the water.

"Well, Feefeen, you did tell Mameen you wanted a new pair of boots," Dolleen laughed.

"That's not funny Dolleen," Feefeen growled.

Captain Brutumus threw the boot back into the water.

"Feefeen it's okay. We'll just try again and maybe this time you'll have better luck," Captain Brutumus said.

"If you're lucky Feefeen, you might catch the other boot," Dolleen laughed.

"Dolleen, start up the engine," Captain Brutumus shouted.

"Aye, aye Captain!"

"Dolleen, I'll steer for a while. You try to catch a fish. Here's your fishing rod," Captain Brutumus smiled.

"I'll just check on Dad first," Dolleen grinned. She went into the cabin. Her Dad was fast asleep on the couch.

"Dolleen I think I have another bite," Feefeen said, as she came back on deck.

"It's probably another old boot," Dolleen laughed.

"Dolleen I need help," Feefeen shouted.

Dolleen grabbed the fishing rod. She was pulled to the edge of the boat.

"Oh Feefeen, it must be a really big fish" she said.

They held the rod and wound the line in.

Suddenly, a big, blue head popped up from the water. The hook from Feefeen's line was in its mouth.

"Wow!" Feefeen yelled. "It's huge!"

Two dolphins suddenly jumped out of the water.

Feefeen and Dolleen fell back, still holding the rod. The dolphins were very big.

"Don't you dare touch my baby! How dare you try to hurt my family," the father dolphin said.

"Dolleen, did that dolphin just speak?" Feefeen gasped.

"He did," Dolleen whispered.

"I will give you five seconds to release my baby or I will sink your boat," the mother dolphin said.

"Let me go," the baby dolphin cried.

"I am very sorry," Feefeen said.

He pulled the baby dolphin onto the boat. He gently took the hook out of its mouth. The dolphin dived back into the sea.

"Please do not sink our uncle's boat," Dolleen cried.

"We won't because you released our baby," the mother dolphin said.

The three dolphins swam off.

As soon as they were gone, Feefeen and Dolleen rushed over to Captain Brutumus. He was behind the steering wheel.

"Uncle Brutumus you won't believe what just

happened. Feefeen caught a baby dolphin. Then its parents said they would sink our boat if we didn't release her," Dolleen said.

"Hold on there now. Where is this baby dolphin?" he asked.

They pulled him over to the other side of the boat.

Captain Brutumus peered over the side. All he could see was the silent, blue sea.

"Are you playing tricks on your Captain?" he asked.

"No Captain! There really were three dolphins," Feefeen and Dolleen shouted.

The Captain just laughed.

Feefeen spotted a large boat coming towards them.

"Look Captain Brutumus, there is a boat coming," he said. "Maybe he saw them."

"That looks like old Peepeen's boat. I wonder what he's doing out here," Captain Brutumus said.

The old boat pulled up beside them.

Captain Peepeen, an old grizzly bear, waved at them.

"Morning all! I'm surprised to see you out today Brutumus," he said.

"I am taking my nephew and my niece on a fishing trip. Bumble has also joined us."

"I remember him well, your sister's husband. Not a sea-lover but one of the fiercest bears I have ever had the pleasure to meet."

"Why are you out this way?"

"I'm on my way back in. Don't you know there is a bad storm coming?

"I know Peepeen, I know. I'm just bringing the young ones to see the mermaids. After that, I'll head back to shore," he smiled.

"Make sure you do Brutumus. Storms have no respect for boats or fisher-folk... no matter how good a sailor they may be. May the wind be at your back," Captain Peepen said, as he sailed away.

"May the seven seas protect you Peepeen," Captain Brutumus shouted back.

Captain Brutumus steered the boat towards some big rocks.

"What's a mermaid, Captain Brutumus?" Feefeen asked.

"Mermaids are the most beautiful creatures in the world. Many fisher-folk are afraid of them. They only ever swim and live in deep water. We are going to their favourite swimming place."

"Why are fisher-folk afraid of them?" Dolleen asked.

"Some folk believe that mermaids are magical creatures," he smiled. "Will we have lunch first?"

The two cubs nodded immediately.

"Aye, aye Captain Brutumus," Feefeen replied.

"Dolleen, will you ask your Dad to join us?"

Dolleen nodded and scampered off to the cabin. She opened the door and saw that he was still asleep.

She ran back. Feefeen and Captain Brutumus were eating fish and munching apples.

"He's asleep so I didn't wake him up," she said.

Captain Brutumus threw Dolleen an apple.

"Your Dad has the loudest snore I've ever heard!" They all started laughing.

"How long have you been a fisherman Uncle Brutumus?" she asked.

"Did your Mameen not tell you that story?" Captain Brutumus laughed.

"No she didn't say anything," Feefeen said.

"Probably afraid you will leave school and run off to join your Uncle Brutumus on the high seas. Dolleen, I have been a fisherman for over 30 years and I have enjoyed every day of my life but I'll let your Mameen tell you about it," Uncle Brutumus said, with a big grin. "Here we are now.

They walked over to the side of the boat and looked down. There was a mermaid in the water.

"Aren't they beautiful?" Captain Brutumus said. And they are very friendly. Good morning Esmerelda."

"Good morning Captain," she said.

"Hello Esmerelda," Feefeen and Dolleen waved.

"Hello cubs!" Esmerelda smiled back.

"I am delighted to meet you," Feefeen grinned.

"Is this the first time you have seen a mermaid?" she asked.

"Yes you are the first!" they shouted.

"And what do you think of mermaids, now that you have met one?"

"You are so beautiful," Dolleen smiled.

"Thank you," Esmerelda laughed.

Mandarin, another mermaid, swam up to the boat.

"Brutumus, a fierce storm is brewing. It is time you went home," Mandarin said.

"Thank you Mandarin," Captain Brutumus said. "We will do just that."

"Well children, it's time for you to leave, but please come back some day," Esmerelda said.

Feefeen and Dolleen nodded and smiled. They waved goodbye.

"The sooner you are back in port, the safer you all will be from the storm. May the seven seas protect you," Mandarin said.

Then the mermaids dived into the sea and swam away.

Captain Brutumus turned the boat around.

Suddenly the engine spluttered and went dead.

The weather began to change. It started to rain heavily and there was a big wind.

"Don't be scared cubs. We'll be alright. Dolleen, hold the wheel and keep steering straight ahead," Captain Brutumus ordered.

Dolleen tried to control the wheel, as the weather got worse. It was very windy and the rain hit her in the face.

"Feefeen come below with me and we'll have a look at the engine. But first get a life-jacket and give it to your father. He's too sea-sick to be any help. It can be hard to tell what a storm will do and it's better to be safe than sorry!" Captain Brutumus said.

"Aye, aye Captain," they shouted.

Feefeen got a life-jacket and ran over to the cabin. Bumble was still fast asleep. He looked very pale. Feefeen gently placed a life-jacket around his shoulders. Bumble kept snoring. Then Feefeen skidded down to the engine.

Captain Brutumus was busy working on it. Feefeen helped by passing him tools. After a few minutes the Captain got it started again.

"I'll finish up here Feefeen. You go and help Dolleen at the wheel," he smiled.

"Aye, aye Captain! This is a great adventure," Feefeen shouted.

He ran up to the steering wheel and helped Dolleen.

Huge waves began to hit the boat. It was thrown up and down on the waves, like a leaf.

"Thanks cubs, I'll take over the wheel now. Stay right beside me," the Captain said.

The wind blew and the boat rocked.

WHOOSH! A huge wind hit the boat and it tilted over. It was falling into the water.

"Feefeen, quick, get your father," Captain Brutumus said.

Feefeen held onto the rail and crawled towards the cabin. But before he reached it, the ship tilted on to its other side.

"Ahhh! I'm sliding back towards the wheel," Feefeen shouted.

"Hold on tight cubs. Feefeen come back here. We need to abandon ship. I'll get Bumble," Captain Brutumus said.

But suddenly the ship popped back out of the water.

"How did that happen?" the Captain asked.

Feefeen crawled over to the side of the boat. He looked into the water. Three dolphins were pressed against the side of the boat.

"Captain, there are three dolphins keeping the boat straight," he shouted.

"What?" Captain Brutumus yelled.

Dolleen slid across to the other side of the boat.

"There are three dolphins on this side too and the baby dolphin," Dolleen shouted. "They are making sure that the boat doesn't fall over."

"Come and look Captain!" Feefeen grinned.

Brutumus was amazed when he saw the dolphins.

"In all my years on the seven seas this is the strangest thing I have ever seen," he said.

As they got near land, the storm began to quieten down. The waves got smaller.

The dolphins moved away from the boat. They started jumping in front of it.

"You saved our lives," Feefeen shouted. "Thank you, thank you."

Captain Brutumus and Dolleen waved and smiled at them.

"Oooh thank you, thank you for saving us," Dolleen yelled.

"You saved the life of our daughter so we got some of our family to help us to save you," the father dolphin said. "Now we must be on our way. And remember the sea can be a very dangerous place."

The dolphins all jumped out of the water at the same time. They waved goodbye with their flippers. Then they all swam away.

"We'd better make sure your father is okay," Captain Brutumus smiled.

They walked into the cabin. Bumble was still asleep! Captain Brutumus nudged him a few times.

Bumble finally woke up with a snort. He sat up and wiped his eyes

"Where am I? I must have fallen asleeeeep. Did you catch any fish yet?"

CPSIA information can be obtained at www.ICGtesting.com
Printed in the USA
LVOW10*1424060214

ROOKMOBILE
JERSEY CITY FREE PUBLIC LIBRARY
472 NEWARK AVENUE
JERSEY CITY, NEW JERSEY 07306
201-547-5503